T0374188

Crazy Love

PATRICIA FAISON-HESTER

authorHOUSE

AuthorHouse™
1663 Liberty Drive
Bloomington, IN 47403
www.authorhouse.com
Phone: 1 (800) 839-8640

Published by AuthorHouse 08/15/2018

ISBN: 978-1-5462-2691-8 (sc)
ISBN: 978-1-5462-2690-1 (e)

In fond remembrance of
My much loved grand-babies

Aniyah Hope Drennon
November 16th - 20th, 2013

and

Reginald Eugene Faison, Jr.
September 21st - 25th, 2004

Acknowledgement

To my family whose love and support has always been my foundation which has allowed me to move forward to new and exciting challenges.

I am thankful to God and family fore their never-ending love and encouragement as I proudly dedicate my second book to them.

Message from the Author

My goal in life is to do that which pleases God and in doing so my family is proud. To see their smile brings me joy; fore, their happiness is my reward.

As you read through my short stories and poems I hope you enjoy them as much as I did in writing them.

I am thankful to God fore many things and of course, the completion of my second book.

"Crazy Love"

Regards

Patricia Faison-HesTer

Dedication – Discipline - Determination

With GOD all things are possible

Matthew 19:26

Contents

My Mom – My Mentor

It saddens my heart that you're not here

It's tough to live my days without you

Fore you were the one I could count on

My rock, my mountain, my foundation

My unwavering truth

As the days come and go

I pray you hear me when I talk to you

Fore when the rain falls

I hope you are not weeping

Fore when I am sleeping, I quietly weep fore you

As I hope, you are not sad

And I pray you're never alone

May our God hold your hand as only he can

As he journeys with you through the upper room

Every day I think of you as I remember the days

When we would sit and chat

Sipped hot coffee and shared our thoughts

I learned so much from you

My independence, my views, my character

All duplicates you

I am who I am because of you

When I look in the mirror, I see you

Without a doubt, I know I mimic you

You envisioned me to be strong, patient and loving

Conscientious, caring, pristine, humble and wise

Proudly to say, "Tis I am"

All these things and so much more

Fore, I live each day with one wish

And that is to make you smile

So when you look down from heaven

May you stand by the angels with a smile then say;

"Tis My Daughter and Damn Right, I'm Proud"

Fore every day I pray in my heart you will stay

Love you Mom, always

"Tis My Heart To Love Thee"
Loving Memories
Annie Lee Green-Faison-Medlock
March 6th 1925 – December 25th 1994

Abandon – Set Free

As a bird is free on snow top trees

Not quite sure why I am afraid

High above the sky my dreams are of you as we lived in the

comforts of the sun. Love me and soar high with me

Years of passion, years of love; children, cats and dogs, heck

we had it all. You decided to leave without restraint or

regrets and abandon the love you promised

Tis a train wreck in motion; my love soared over a cliff, now

failed and derailed; no air, no survival, no happiness, no life

Why? Why? Why? What happened?

Our lives merged together fore we walked the same path

We made history as we laughed and cried together

We amend the wrong, made it right, and erased confusion

Fore our love was not an illusion as our love was never-ending

Fore you were my life, my love, my heart and soul

Tis you and me true love to behold

In the end, it was to be just the two of us

I'm now solo and I fly alone, Divorced – Sadden and Dismayed

- of course -

Alone I Sit

Here amid the shimmering ocean waters

I sit

What a fantastic view, waters of deep blue

I sit and sit as I think of you

The thought of you makes my heart smile

Sometimes the thought of you bring tears to my eyes

There are times I cry and cry but I shall sit and wait a while

As the cool breeze blows over the seas and along the coastal

front, crashing waves and rushing tides

Fore miles and miles, dark blue waters are all I see

I sit along the water then smile

Fore I know I will forever love thee

Alone I sit and wait fore my brave black shiny knight

With shield in hand he will gallop alongside cool coastal waters

At midnight, he arrives

To comfort me

Beautiful Oak Tree

Century old, standing bold, standing strong, beautifully it stands as it stands alone

Stretching out its branches with leaves of colors; tans and golden browns as it yearns sunlight

Standing on solid ground, the cool stream runs across its path

Leaning low and showing age, oh how this saddens me, layers of life and life's stages have past

What may I ask of this beautiful oak tree? Will it answer me?

I stand beneath and look above, lo and behold, what do I see?

My ancestors looking down at me, tears flow like falling leaves

Can it be this tree bares grief and sorrow?

What have the old oak tree seen? Fore it holds many stories it seems

Beauty is its bark, just like Noah's Ark.

Bold, strong and masculine, stands bravely in front of me

It holds the tales of my ancestry of sweet words of wisdom

Decades long and seasons of life, the tree yearns to tell its secrets to me

Beautiful old oak tree, what truths will you withhold from me?

Body Temp

Cold days, hot nights

Warm and sweaty

Feeling lazy

You drive me crazy

Sweet kisses, tight hugs

Strong hands, soft fingers

Love me all night

Cold days, hot nights

Warm and sweaty

Wet sheets, sweet sweat

Black skin

Love me, love me

All night

Thick lips, tight thighs

I'm under your spell

I'm under your skin

Love me, hold me

You drive me crazy

Cold days, hot nights

Love me all night

Creatures of the Dark

Come out at night to howl at the moon just before daylight

Creatures of darkness both wicked and vile

Hang out at night just a little while

As they roam to and fro with no place to go

Filled with anger, filled with hate, filled with shame

They are insane

Most don't know their names

They howl at the moon and talk to themselves as they too live in fear

Does anyone care? Fore, they are dangerous to everyone

Distorted are their minds, what has happened to mankind?

Fore they were once children who we loved and consoled

Now they are brutal, cold and unkind; who live in darkness and do crime

Please God have mercy on their souls

They are creatures of the dark who do not sleep

And they give me cause to weep

"No excellent soul is exempt from a mixture of madness"
Aristotle

Cry

I cry out fore my heart is full

Full of fire, full of rage

My soul weeps as my body burns

As I am weak and I cannot stand

So I stumble, slip and fall

Oh, how I yearn to end it all

Fore the seasons have changed, a change in seasons

Winter, spring, summer and fall

Fire, wind, sun and rain

Where do I start, how do I begin

How do I unburden my soul?

Learn to love, love life, and love to live and yearn fore love

Fore I can't stand it; must I crawl, beg and struggle

Darkest shadows left behind

Do I seek and search to find my true love tomorrow

Fore today my heart is all worn out

Tonight I weep and sleep

I pray to love life all over again

At the start of a new day, the sun will rise and so will I

And I will find my true love once again

Enrapture My Love

Lying directly under you, your body touching mine

Naked to nakedness; of course, I feel your warmth

Embrace your scent; cling to your flesh

Kiss your skin as your lips find mine

Rub my thighs as I rub yours, breathe in your ear

Listen, as our heart-beat finds its rhythm

Feel the pounding of your heart as you cling to my soul

To know we each have the same damn goal

To find heaven, ecstasy awaits; as an earthquake rumbles and tumbles us upon warm sheets

We moan and groan like a lion and lioness, we love, hug and kiss

Fill me; touch me, as I explode. Listen closely, as I say your name

My body, your body; from top to bottom, bottom to top

Thanks to heaven there's no clock

Rewind, repeat, and start all over again

Now that's what I call;" Healthy Love"

Fallen From Grace

As I filter through space, I glide and I fly as I take a nose dive. Not sure of the time; yet, I'm falling fast

Spinning and spinning, amid thin air, I flutter, I sputter and spin till I drop; hope not to crash and burn when I stop

Though I have something to learn, so I try to hang on fore, my heart has been torn and of course, I am scorned

As I have fallen from grace. I flutter along, hanging in space Only to be caught by the brave bald eagle

His claws grip me ever so tight, as he soars higher and higher. Wings spans two feet wide and I cannot see beyond fore, I dangled in mid-air and yes I am afraid. Afraid to let go; I look below, I see my ego

Exposed are my errors, exposed are my sorrows, exposed are my guilt, exposed are my sinful days

Flying high, I can only wish fore tomorrow; fore, the eagle will soon let me go, as I have fallen from grace

There is no way to erase; my past, my sorrows, and my hate, or my ill-gotten ways

My only wish; if I cannot fly with the eagles then I shall clean up my act and hold my head high

Then maybe tomorrow, I'll fly with the sparrows

Until I mend my ways

Family Jewels

Is it pearls or is it land?

Possibly its money

Or the seed planted in my mother's womb

First day on earth, my birth name given

That passes on from generation to generation

My family jewels move slowly along the continent Africa

Like soil that has been toiled; my name lives on

As the seed grows and the Nile River flows

My family name rises with the morning sun

And moves along the river in darkness and light

Then lay its burdens upon rocks at midnight

As a misty cloud releases its morning dew

It enriches and strengthens my family tree

A new era begins at birth

And the seed from my family jewels form a genetic heirloom

That will someday return to our rightful nation

Africa

Fat Belly

Soft like jelly, warm and fluffy

And yet it's cuddly

Oh, it's his belly

Squeeze him tightly

Soft as a marsh-mellow

My favorite pillow

Fluffy and soft

This should be outlawed

Fore this is the best

My very best head-rest

Hands on his chest

Cuddle up, snuggle up, and cozy up

Hug him tight

A few more kisses

And

I'll sleep soundly tonight

Fear Within

I am not so good a naturalist (as they call it) as to discern what secret creates fear as this emotion lies deep within all of us; but, be this as it may. "Tis it odd how fear lives within us as it can or may distort our views, our dreams, our reality"?

"Of fears," I have many, but one stands out more than the others. My memory of my earliest fear is drowning. As a child of age four or five, I clearly remember waking up in the middle of the night screaming at the top of my lungs, calling out in my loudest voice for my sleeping mother to awake and save me from this terror. In my dream there was my older sister Clara and I was returning home from school. As we walked home, my sister said, "Come lets go this way, this is a quicker route to home;" and as we turned the corner we stepped into a huge ocean wave and the ocean wave was as high as mountains. The water swept us apart and I could no longer see her. I lost sight of my sister in the ocean waters. I began to drown. I'm now under water bubbles and bubbles, down, down and down I went into the darkness and I could not swim. I could hear myself screaming for my sister calling her name out loudly until I could scream no more. "Clara," "Clara," "Clara," "please come back." I'm scared, I freeze in the moment. Suddenly, I was awakened by my mother who had shaken me from my sleep. She assured me that my sister Clara was just across from me sleeping. Mom held me close as I fell quietly back to sleep. But, I knew in my heart this dream had placed a fear in me and I would never fully recover from the terror of this dream. I became very fearful of ocean waters, swimming pools, lakes and even full bathtubs of water. The horror of drowning never left me and neither did the fear.

As I grew older, the fear continued to live strongly inside me and it has never left me.

You see my high school friend went snorkeling in the ocean of Florida's coast during our high school senior trip when tragedy hit. A group of students, including my friend Khandee were snorkeling while I waited at the coconut beverage stand for their return. As I waited for their return I began to giggle to myself as to how Khandee and I first met.

We were in the first grade at the time and I had joined the Art class. We were all seated in class when I realized a girl sitting right next to me and she was staring. She was watching my every move. When I looked at her to figure out why she was staring, she then stuck out her tongue. Of course, I was surprised at this behavior but, heck we were in the first grade so I stuck my tongue out right back at her. So she rolled her eyes and turned her head as she made a clicking sound with her tongue. As I heard the teacher in the back ground talking I waited for the girl to look my way again so I could roll my eyes too but instead, I gave her a crossed-eyed look then we burst into laughter. The teacher gave me a look but it was a warning look. But I could not stop laughing and thinking as who is this silly girl who sitting right next to me. I thought who is this fool? As we tried to control our laughter it proved impossible. We were warned again by the teacher. Later when she thought the teacher wasn't looking she passed me a note that said. "What's your name? I wrote down "Trish" then passed the note back. She wrote her name Khandee then returned it but she had crossed out Trish and wrote the word, Butter. I looked up at her but this time stranger than before, then she started laughing saying I should call you Butter because that's your skin color. So I said, "Sure and I'll call you

Coco" cause you look like chocolate milk; we laughed and laughed. This time the teacher gave us another warning saying she would send us to the office if we continue to talk. From that day on we were inseparable. We were like two peas in a pod. We walked home together that afternoon and I learned we lived two blocks apart, so from then on we would walk to school every day together.

Khandee never grew in height much as we got older and her dress size was only a size four, but boy could she eat. For the amount of food she ate you would think she would be fatter. But instead she was like an energized bunny with bright eyes and short bangs. As a teenager she hated her looks because of her hazel green eyes. She would say no one would ever marry her because of her eyes but we laughed and said it was because of her appetite. She simply loved food, she loved to eat and she never gained a pound. She stood five feet even and I was five feet three inches. She was also daring and willing to take on challenges. As we got older, if one of the other children challenged her to a jump rope contest, a race to see who could run the fastest, or to see who could swing the highest on the swing set, she would take on the challenge. Khandee would take on a challenge without hesitation. Khandee loved to swim in the neighborhood pool at our local playground. She always asked me to go swimming with her and our friends but I always refused.

I remember one day as we were doing homework and out of the blue she asked if I thought we would be friends forever. I replied of course. So; she insisted we do a pinky swear and of course, we roared with laughter. We both made funny faces as we confirmed our friendship through a pinky swear. She was truly a child comedian. We always laughed and laughed till our sides ached and our eyes were filled with tears. She could come out of the blue with the weirdest things. I was the book-worm as I would read everything; books, magazines, encyclopedias, newspapers, candy wrappers, and cereal boxes you name it my eyes were glued to it. I borrowed so many books from the library that the librarian knew my name. She would say in her soft yet squeaky voice "Trish how many books are you borrowing today? Khandee would turn around to imitate the librarian as the librarian would say to Khandee "young lady why aren't you getting any books today"? And Khandee would frown then say, "I lost my library card". Khandee was crossing her fingers as she made that statement. As soon as we were outside we would laugh and laugh. Khandee walked very fast and I walked slowly. Her mother said; "We were complete opposites and could not understand how we were best friends".

So here, I am waiting at the coconut beverage stand and time had passed. Then I saw a group of students and asked if they saw Khandee and they replied "no". I continued to wait as I heard another group of students laughing and giggling but still Khandee had not arrived. So I asked again, "Has anybody seen my friend Khandee?" and "Do you know where she is"? Then, someone shouted, "No, they had not seen her."

Then that dreadful thought came to my mind; my horrible dream. I then tried very hard not to panic, telling myself don't panic, don't panic. I repeated she'll show up, she'll show up. I thought maybe she went further down the Ocean walk and was probably just tired from swimming and was walking slowly towards the Cocoanut stand. But, as time passed, I could no longer wait, I burst into tears. I ran frantically towards the other end of the beach hoping and praying to meet her. My gut instinct told me something was wrong. I ran for what felt like a half mile searching and calling out my friend's name. "Khandee," "Khandee," I screamed and cried. "Khandee" oh my God, please, please, where is she? I yelled, and I yelled Khandee. Soon my classmates joined in, I heard them behind me scream and yell out her name too, but to no avail, my friend Khandee never answered. So the students and I ran for help. We ran as hard and as fast as possible to find teachers, chaperons and aides telling anybody we passed to help look for her.

Upon hearing our story authorities were quickly notified. The policemen were alerted, expert scuba divers searched the ocean as my classmates and I waited in terror. We prayed for Khandee's return. I remember standing there hoping, wishing and praying that this was a bad dream, but of course it was not. I stood there frozen in time, frozen in fear while kicking myself fore I could not stop thinking I should have learned to swim. My questions were; "Was I supposed to die? Was I supposed to be the one who drowned in the ocean's water instead of Khandee?" As we waited and waited for answers I cried as I questioned myself as why was this happening.

Khandee was found many hours later and many miles away from her entry point of the ocean. Her cause of death was classified as "Drowned" and reason for death "Accidental Drowning". Though it was unclear how she was not noticed by anyone while in the waters. The only explanation provided was the possibility of a huge undercurrent that could have swept her under the ocean waters which gave her petite body no chance to surface for air or no chance of survival. They noted that the undercurrents could pull a house under water for the ocean waters are very strong and very unpredictable.

On the plane ride home every student mourned for my friend and classmate. We grieved and mourned my friend Khandee as we headed home without her. The plane was so quiet that the only sounds were heard was the sniffles and tears of the students. September 28th was a very sad day for all.

As time passed the fear within and the sadness never allowed me to discuss what happened openly. My mother tried very hard to comfort me but my sadness would not leave me. I tried to forget that day. I tried to erase it from all memory. I always felt had I not been so afraid of water the terrible accident may not have happened. Just maybe, I could have convinced her not to go out so far into the ocean. Maybe her death could have been prevented. This was a horrible tragedy, but it was my nightmare. It was the nightmares that repeated and repeated many times as a child yet, somehow my childhood nightmare came true.

Years later, many of my friends suggested that I take swimming lessons. As Montaigne writes "dethrone" or conquer your fear. My fears are of ocean waters and maybe just learning to swim could possibly help heal my broken heart over losing my friend. But for now, "Fear Within" has triumph.

As I write these pages I tremble and cry with fear and sadness because I cannot dethrone my fear of ocean water, lakes and rivers. But more importantly I can never forgive myself nor forget my friend, my best friend Khandee and our pinky swear.

"Friends Forever"

Fear Within to be continued. Is truly a story written from the author's imagination. The fictitious names and characters are all parts and roles of the author's creative writing.

Few Letters

Few letters
One word
LOVE

Few thoughts
One idea
DREAM

Pair of lips
One mouth
KISS

Two arms
One body
HUG

Two eyes
Focus
On ME

Your voice
One song
SING

Two hands
One GOD
PRAY

One heart
Countless heart-beats
TIS ME

Friend

Worry not my friend, fore the door is open and never closes

You're never alone fore he's always there with an attentive ear

The one you can depend on as he's the one to call on

So raise your hands, give praise, and call out his holy name

Thanks to thee, a friend indeed

Bow your head and bend your knees, clap your hands

Say Father please; bless his holy name

Fore we call him JESUS

Thanks be to GOD

Fore he is here

Never to forsake you nor let you down

He consistently awaits you fore he is always around

So hold onto his word then stand firm

Fore you stand on solid ground

Gather in prayer fore he is there

Merciful, powerful, blessed is he

Fore his light of love shines eternally

Praise his holy name, his word, his works

Fore sure, fore certain; you have a friend, a father, a kin

My GOD, Our Father, GOD of all

My Holy Father, my very best friend

Gentle Giant

On the shoulders of a gentle giant I stand

The man who holds my hand

Tall, dark and black he is, smile bright as sunlight

True, I love this giant of a man as he holds my hand

I walk and skip to school each day, tired and exhausted from

long day of recess and play

Cookies and milk my favorite treats we are heading home

fore mommy has cooked us something to eat

Gently the giant lifts me towards the sky as he swings me high

in the air; like a bird I fly

Screaming and laughing I cried "don't' let go, don't let go" he

promised to love me till the day I die. Happily and lovingly I

smile at the sky fore this loving giant was my

Pop pop pop pop; I hear crackling gun shots

This dreadful day my gentle giant fell to the ground; random

bullets had his name on it. He fell to the ground, straight on

his back, flat as a pancake with no backpack. Tightly I held

onto his hand as I screamed and cried there I fell upon my

giant's chest. I cried, he smiled then he said; "I love you my

sweet child". I screamed and cried with tears in my eyes as I

asked; "Why"? Who would want to hurt my gentle giant? Fore

no-one loved my gentle giant but mommy and me. Across the street not very far there stood in the shadows a woman and she smiled at me. She dropped a gun then covered her face. Why? I asked, "Did she hurt my gentle giant"? Someone yelled, she is a dirty bleep bleep scorned side chick.

Low and behold the gentle giant was laid to rest.

Here today, the pain of the gentle giant lay heavy upon my chest.

My gentle giant was my daddy and I loved him the best.

Memories now lay heavy upon my breast.

Tears from heaven fore I know he cries; I feel the warmth of his smile saying "Hold on baby girl, don't let go; fore I love you forever, heart and soul".

Hair

Looking real fly

Dangling curls falling

Way pass my eyes

Soft to the touch

Draped past my shoulders

Long in length

Hair that flows

Everyone knows

It's fake

It's a weave

It's my hair

Don't cost much

Got it half price

Two for one sale

Rocking honey golden blonde

Ain't I fine?

Can't you see?

It's all mine

Hey Honey

Honey where's my money?

          What money, honey?

You know the money I lent you

          Oh baby that was spent

Spent on what?

          Spent on the rent

Oh no
You paid that too

          Well yeah, it was due

Oh no, I paid it too

          You paid it too?

Oh no, Now what we gonna do?

          I wish I knew

Hey honey

          Yeah

I love you

          Babe, I am watching the game

Hold Me Gently

Hold me gently in your arms

Keep me safe

And keep me warm

Tell you love me all night long

Assure me I will never be alone

And through the storms

Forever hold me tight

Share your dreams with me day and night

Whisper sweet words of love

As we journey through life

Forever and ever

I shall be yours

Till the end of daylight

May your day be as

LOVELY

as your first sip of hot tea

Hot Tea

Mmmmmmmmh, herbal tea

Let's see, smells nice I just might have a cup

Assorted flavors, lemon honey, mint, green, raspberry

And several more I have not tried

Smell so good as steam rises from my perfect red cup

I think I'll take three small sips

Mmmmmmh just what I thought, delicious

The aroma relaxes my mind and soothes my inner soul

So I sit, relax, stretch my legs and settle down

Mental note: What God has done fore me

Sipped my tea and cleared my head

Focus on my Lord, as I pray my Lord is please with me

You see;

Life ain't so bad

Fore I am thankful fore the love of my family

As I know my blessings and I am thankful to God

I raise my teacup high in the air

A toast to my LORD "PRAISE", I say

In this life I have had plenty and thankful to thee

Fore my Lord has been good to me

Husband

I love the six feet man of mine

I am his lady and his wife, nothing is more satisfying

Then to lie in his arms as he whispers in my ear of his love and

how he adores me. Tints of gray hairs warmly shadows his chin

His power and strength enfolds me

Fore which I love as he touches and holds me

He is my man and I love him profoundly,

Dressed in the finest of suits, name brand shoes and ties

Looking real good and smelling real nice

Damn; he is fine and of course, he is mine

His presence surrounds me even after the sun has gone down

Fore he is the love of my life

We share the same name and we share many things

Loving him has brought me much joy and happiness

I pray to live in his heart forever more

And may I always be the **ROSE** in his garden that never die

Fore in his heart is where I lie

As I run my fingers through the tints of gray hairs on his chin

My love grows and grows deeper within

Tis my love, to love my husband forever, and ever

Fore **"I AM"** his wife

I'm Cute

I'm sexy

I 'm plump

And curvy

I'm vanilla

I'm caramel

I'm sweet to the taste

You can honey dip

My chocolate

As you squeeze my marsh mellows

You see

I freeze

I melt

And smooth to the touch

With different size cups

My flavors are like rainbows

Hey, STOP; stop drooling

And control your self

Cut it out

I'm ice cream

Arise, shine fore thy light is come

And the glory of the LORD

Is risen upon thee

Isaiah 60:1

I Rise

It's a new day

Thank GOD I pray

Then

I'm on my way,

Thank GOD I'm feeling good

Standing strong

Mind is clear

Got plenty of sleep

I'm gonna take the world on

Few friends

Money in the bank

The Lord has been good to me

Early morning, it's a new day

With a plan in hand, I stand

and

I rise

Journey

A walk in the park

A stroll in the dark

Run down the hills

Skip through the valley

Climb up the mountains

Visited caves and caverns

A trot by the ocean

A wave by the sea

Drove around the bend

Going north, south and east

You see;

My journey had not been easy

Nor did I get lost fore, I held onto my compass

As I made my way across

Up one way and down the other; never knowing what I'd

discover

A friend here and a lover there; sweetness in the air

Pacing here and racing there, I've been everywhere

I've looked high and I've looked low

My Love, My Love

"Where are you"?

Kiss

Sweet-Sweet with pretty, big lips, yes that's me

That' my name Sweet-Sweet I am sweeter than ice tea

Mmmmmmmmh oh boy and do I love to kiss

You see: I'm five feet five with really big lips

And bright hazel eyes, nothing is strange about me

But don't fore a minute think I'm not sweet

I got what I got and I'm Damn hot

Just got big lips and I love to kiss

Kiss, kiss, and kiss me now, Kiss me later. Forget the hugs

Forget the pillow talk. Hell no, I don't like to walk nor hold

hands; all I want to do is sit and smooch

Kiss my forehead, kiss my cheeks

Close your eyes and don't you peek. Kiss my lips

Oh yeah, kiss my neck mmmmmmmmh that feels nice

Pucker up baby and kiss me again

When you are tired and need fresh air

Take a break and I'll wait right here; ready to start all over

again. Fore my lips are big and always ready

To kiss you over and over again

Kiss, kiss, and kiss

That's me Sweet-Sweet just like ice tea

Kneel Before GOD

Hair tangled and so out of place

Puffy eyes filled with water, tears rolled down my face;

Silently I sobbed

Could not help myself; I had to cry

Fore my life was turned upside down, shaken apart and

tossed around. There I stood on cracked glass and shaky

ground

I looked towards heaven and loudly I cried

Pleaded to the LORD, please save this broken-hearted child

Poured my heart out and sang a song

As the warm sun touched my face, I saw clearly the sky was

blue and I knew then I was in God's grace.

I heard him say, "Be bless my child"

My eyes dried and I smiled

Fore I remembered I was his child.

And in due time, GOD's time

I would heal and walk on steady ground

Fore love is blind and cannot see

At that very moment, I learned there is no guarantee

"That fore whom I loved may not love me"

Knight

Dark knight, dark knight

My heart is light

Fore I found the love of my life

The scent of my man is present

My lips, his lips we gently kiss

Strong arms hold me close

Our hearts are full with love

My head held high as I walk by his side

Safe and sound I am, tightly he squeezed my hand

Left hand, gold band holds onto my right

Hand in hand, synchronized we step,

Proudly from day to day

I smile, he smile

My knight has paved our way

With love

Delight yourself in the LORD and he will give
you
the desires of your heart.

Psalm 37:4

LORD

My burdens are heavy

And the waters are deep

Sometimes I sit and cry

And simply cannot sleep

Lord

You know my pain

and my uncertainties too

lighten my spirit

lift my heart

shelter me from harm

wipe away my tears

restore my strength

bless my soul

then grant me wisdom with a tab bit of courage

hold my hand and walk with me

fore I know I'm not alone

AMEN

Love

I love you, I love you, I love you

And I will say it everyday

I love you even if you cannot say

Fore I'm okay

I'm fine with it

I'm happy that I said it

I love you and

I love me, myself and I

Loving me means loving you less

So when I look into the mirror

Here's what I see

The one who needs my love

Is me loving me

Now that I said it:

I'm happy with it

Happily loving me

Lovingly

I placed my hand on his hand

He kissed it; he then kissed my lips

He held me close as tears filled my eyes

He kissed my tears then said,

"Don't cry"

I cried and he smiled

He held my hand

Kissed my lips

Hugged my hips

Declared his love

Over and over again

I cried, he smiled then said

"No fear, "I'm here

To love and provide fore you

My birthright as King is to protect my Queen

As you and me, share my throne forever

Man Down

Pound fore pound

Dear Lord, my man is taking a beating

I pray he can go one more round

Oh no; he takes a knee, referee counts: one, two, three.....

Quickly he stands and nods his head

Referee said a few words, ok; then the fight proceeds

My man is holding his own, ducking and moving

Geeze that's great I waged a fortune on him

Baby needs shoes and my rent is due

My man shifts to the left and then to right

Damn, I thought this was going to be an easy fight

But my man just caught one in the eye

So he throws off a jab and then a straight right hook

Bobbing and weaving, sweat everywhere

Blood dripping here and there, swollen lips, puffy eyes

Oh boy, Can my man see?

His feet imitates the shuffle of the greatest fighter

of an early era; again he bobs and weaves

Got his man on the ropes, oh yeah

This might be the round, maybe?

My man pounds and pounds on his opponent truly hard

Punch after punch he throws but the opponent is a good

fighter and yet, he won't take a knee

Oh my goodness, blood and sweat everywhere;

I feel faint

Screaming and yelling I yell "Baby go, Baby go" Baby. Oh NO

Uh oh, down went the opponent

Looks like my man might get a win

Fore tonight's fight could be his first night as

"Heavyweight Champion"

I cross my fingers and close my eyes

then start to say a prayer or two

My man head to his corner as the opponent was looked over

The ring doctor waves his hands out wide, the crowd roars

Oh boy, what do I see? A white towel tossed into the ring,

Damn, Damn, this I can't believe

Oh yeah, oh yeah, I scream out loud, that's a wrap,

That's a win

fore

My man, my baby and me

"The Heavyweight Champion of the World", loves me

Moment

One moment in the morning

One moment at night

Can't you see?

I'm ready and ripe

As I move elegantly beneath the cool waters of the night

Willingly and anxiously ready to bite

Drop your line to see if I strike

Hang around here

There will be fried fish

Fore dinner tonight

Monday – Monday

Monday morning the perfect day

I love it, my favorite day of the week

Weekend is over and it's back to work

Ready to share my thoughts and views

With coworkers, friends and even you

Of weekend events and how it was spent

Someone will call out sick; others will avoid the day

Or show up late fore their car won't start

But, Oh no, not me; happy as a lark that's me

Can't wait to share my weekend stories to put everyone
in a roar

Bring in laughter and raise their eyebrows too

When I tell them how my dog had the farts

Smelled up the house and chased us all out

We will settle in as our week begins

To sip on coffee, hot chocolate or tea

Monday – Monday the perfect day fore me

Night Flight

On the plane I fly

Silently I sit and cry fore quiet is the ride

Long is this flight although I'm not going far

Not to Rome, Japan or even Africa

What I thought when I booked the ride was a simple short

flight to Las Vegas

Wrong I was fore this is such a long flight

As I cannot wait to land, so silently I cry

Deep within I sigh fore I am eager to land

If only someone was here to hold my hand

Next time I will execute a plan

Head north

Then drive to Canada

No More Lies

On my way home, short of a dime, got any change?
he replied, I'm all out

Mmmm, the dish is delish, got a recipe to share?
Tis a family secret and you're not an heir

Running late - In need of a ride
Sorry to say, don't break your stride
I'm not going your way

All shucks, I like those shoes, got a few bucks
Where did you buy them?
Don't know, my man bought these
Awh geeze, just my luck

Nice dress suit, did you buy it?
        Nope; it's tailor made,
        I got it from the shop
Down-town shop? Nope
Up-town shop? Nope
        My sister's shop, she made it, she sews

He's a sharp dresser
        Where does he work?
He doesn't
He manages her

It's lunchtime, want something to eat?
        Nah, I already ate
You already ate?
        Yep, I ate my lunch at breakfast

Power

Power of love

Moves from love to hate

Hate you in the morning

Love you all night

There is no reason

Like jersey tomatoes

We are plum out of season

From summer to winter

All has turned cold

Loved you at first sight

Oh well, what the hell

Our relationship is corrupt

Its time

Time is up

Ran Like Hell

Walking down the street one day with not much to say, didn't give it thought but nothing was going my way. I cleared my head fore, it was a warm sunny day when I heard footsteps close behind. I turned around to see what was trailing me. Oh no! What did I see? It was the got damn devil and he was grinning at me. I stepped to my right. He stepped to his left. Fore sure he scared the hell out of me. He looked me straight in my eyes; he smiled and I cried. He said, "Take my hand and come with me fore, I've got lots and lots fore you to see". With tears in my eyes I said, "Hell to the No", I don't wanna die". The mere thought of death makes me cry. Why would I go? There's not a got damn thing in hell that I wanna see. So please, please, leave me be.

He smiled then frowned and said. "You're going with me". I took one step back, turned around and ran like hell. As I ran, and ran I prayed to find some place to hide; fore, the devil scared the crap out of me.

I screamed and yelled and "Hell to the No"; I didn't scream fore ice cream.

I ran and ran then I walked and walked trying hard to clear my thoughts. I turned around, no devil was near. Found a place where I could sit and rest a while. Panting and wheezing I tried to catch my breath; looked around as I was scared to death. And oh boy, what did I see? "Hell to the No", I was deep down below.

Underground; underground, far, far below, the very place I did not wanna go. What the hell? What did I see? Oh no; there was a got damn dead man staring at me. Six feet underground, underground there I cried, stood knee-deep in hell with bones and skulls up to my thighs. Thick clouds of smoke blinded me. Faint voices from afar screamed out "Please help me".

I said; "Hell to the No"; this is not for me. This ain't where I wanna be. Hot gravel, melting rocks, smoke and dirt; damn I cried, scared to death, I was horrified and I could not breathe. Then I hollered, "What the hell is that smell? There was darkness everywhere and it looked like the devil had his eyes on me; I took one step back turned around and ran like hell.

I ran and ran then walked and walked until I could run no more. No sign of the devil and not much else to see, shaken to my bones I screamed "Somebody, please help me". There were empty roads full of dirt, dust and no sign of life; air of death and ghost towns, I wondered, how can this be? Everything haunted and deserted. My thought, if only I could find my way home. So I closed my eyes then clicked my heels and counted to three as I softly whispered "home, home, I wanna go home". Open my eyes, looked around, here now that got damn trick did not work fore me. Now I had no clue what I was gonna do.

Weary and tired and truly exhausted, I slowly approached the end of the road. Right then and there what did I see? Some old ugly haggard and she was staring at me. She was smoking and grinning as she stirred her black pot. I asked, "What's that you got?" She replied, "Pot Luck". She scooped her ladle and licked her lips, drooled at the mouth then took a sip. She looked into my eyes then winked at me. Scared me to the bones so I whispered, "What's your thoughts and what do you see"?

She said with a smile, "Something for you my sweet child". I know you been running and running and can't find your way. So here's a tip, take that road then turn left, three stops down, make a quick right then you'll see a hanging light; that's where you'll meet your undertaker. Hurry now, be there by midnight.

I shook my head and cried and cried, "Hell to the No; "I don't wanna hear that". I took one step back turned around and ran like hell. I ran and ran then walked and walked trying to clear my head when I screamed, "This is a got damn dream".

Wheezing and wheezing and gasping for air, I tried to catch my breath; feeling very sad, I sat along the side of the road. No sign of the devil so I laid to rest. Flat on my back, I stretch and yawned, looked around and low and behold, what did I see? An old familiar playground; here I found my old neighborhood.

Liked what I saw, walked in the bar; said Bartender, Bartender; fix me a drink. Bring me wine, whiskey, scotch, and gin then throw in a beer from tap; I wanna sit here and think.

I sipped and sipped, then gulped and gulped, then guzzled my brew and thought and thought, here now I decided to stay.

So I sat and sat then had more drinks fore I wanted to kill some time and not worry about losing my mind. Fore damn sure I didn't wanna think about dying and I was gonna stop the got damn crying. I said, "Bartender, Bartender, bring me more drinks", all I wanna do is clear my head and think.

Said to myself; "Hell to the No", I don't wanna die. It's better for me to sit, drink and think then hang around here a while. Fore, there's no way in hell will I take that road so, let the got damn Undertaker wait for me.

At the bar, I sat in a warm cozy spot and had more drinks as I thanked God fore I was alright and here it seemed this just might be a damn good night. So I order another round of drinks.

I said; Bartender, Bartender bring me more drinks, wine, whiskey, scotch and gin and throw in a beer from tap as I wanna sit here and think.

While feeling good and sipping my drinks, I heard someone sit right next to me, so I looked up, turned around and there was the got damn devil staring at me. You see, he cornered me in the bar and I screamed fore, this was not a got damn dream. He placed his hand on my shoulder then said:

Undertaker, Undertaker, make that three, for you, me and she. He looked me straight in my eyes and said:
"Tag, you're dead and you're going with me"; and I screamed. Then the devil said:

"The trouble is you think you have more time". **Buddha**

Remember

Moment by moment and every hour of the day

I remember clearly how we met that day

I waited fore you to walk my way

Fore, your physique was unique

Toned to the bones, chiseled chest, rock hard abs

Muscular thighs, beautiful skin, handsome grin

Women all went wild

If you were the lottery

My ticket would win

I would have to say your swag was live

Fore sure you had style, you made me smile

We walked a mile as you talked trash

We sipped on brews, laughed out loud

Laughed all night, till sun light

After all these years, it's been you and me

And you haven't changed a bit

Believe it or not, we're still best friends

Secrets

Words not spoken

What is hidden?

Sure is hurting

White lies, dirty secrets, dark nights

Filled with tears, wrapped in fear

My enemy is near

Silent lips, closed minds, all hide the truth

Mysteries and lies, destroying lives,

To add more lies

Corrupt minds, rotten souls,

Gossip triumphs over me

Unburden my soul; may the truth be told

Unveil, unwrap, expose, fully disclose

Set it free

Then of course

Leave me be

Stand By Thee

I am the woman that stands by you

Than how is it you cannot see me

You look at the wall then you look at the floor

You will even look at whoever passes you by

But I am the woman that stands by thee

And I am the woman who pampers and loves you

What do you look fore when you look the other way?

When you look down the hall what do you expect to see?

Fore certain and fore sure, it is not me

Fore I am the woman who stands by thee

But you do not see as there's no sparkle in your eyes

When you look at me, how can that be?

You see, at the moment its evening and the hour is here

With anticipation and jubilation, I hold my toddler's hand

We stand on the front porch as we await his Daddy to come

home after a long day at work

With love,

I smile

Tears in my eyes

I proudly stand by thee

Stand firm
Let nothing move you

1 Corinthians 15:58

Stop

Can everybody please; just stop

Stop the hurt and pain, stop faking and the Got Damn acting

Together lets walk down memory lane; rid your worries and

tell the truth. As I promise your words won't fall on deaf ears.

I see in your eyes that you are hurt; go to church on Sundays,

cry on Mondays, scream on Tuesdays, hush – hush fore the

remainder of the week. It's not ok; it's not ok fore you to

bottle up your pain inside. Come my sisters and let out your

cries. I can't take anymore as I watch you daily as you die

inside. I will not ignore your plea nor pretend I don't see

I will not pretend that you are not a part of my extended
family

We can no longer deny the truth fore its ok that things are

not going your way. It's rare two minds think alike anyway

Rome wasn't built in a day nor kinship but friendship and
sisterhood will last always

So please stop hiding out and share your thoughts

Your torment and pain brings misery to all

Share with me what's on your mind and heart

> Do not be annoyed with yourself or with me
> Fore sharing your thoughts will bring you
> Peace and Harmony

Sunday Morning

Woke up this morning and feeling pretty good

Rose from bed, stretched out my arms

Made a full yawn with sleep in my eyes

I waddled down the hall and off to shower

Outside the rain poured non-stop as the thunder roared

Clacking and cracking the lighting crackled across the sky

If I don't get in and out of the shower quickly

I'll be fried; bleep, bleep

The wind whistled through the trees

Ripping and scratching its beautiful leaves

I dashed from the shower wrapped in a towel

As my wet feet waddled over the warm soft carpet floor

The mighty thunder pounded and pounded beneath the sky

I duck and run with no place to hide

Boom, boom, boom the thunder echos through the house

Though I had planned to attend church

The storm would not let up

So I brushed my hair and laid across my bed

Thunder, lighting and rain I closed my eyes

As I found sleep instead

Soundly I slept through the warm summer storm

When I awake its mid-morning

Time passed, the clock showed it was seven pass eleven

Sunday sermon's fore sure was over

Ran to the window as the sun peered in

It's a total new day from hours' ago

No sign of the rain and the sun is bright

It's a perfect Sunday morning to start my tea pot

I dressed and checked my clock

Mom is waiting fore me as we planned brunch

You see

There's no better way to spend my day

Fore it's Sunday morning

And a day spent with Mom always, always makes it

A wonderful day

Summer

Summer weather

Hot and sticky

Temperature up past 105

Sun's hot, there's no shade

Hate to go outside it's too hot to play

Run the AC all day

Night come I am bored and alone

No fun

No matter the weather

My poem will live on

Forever

Talk To Me

Warm and snuggle inside; I can hear you when you talk to me

Remind me daily you love me

And how you'll always be there to comfort me

Remind me you will forever care and you will always be there

As you wait patiently fore me to arrive

Maybe some night just before dawn or right before your

Coffee brews; fore sure, I will surprise you

So talk to me and or sing me a song,

Or sometimes read me your favorite poem

I love you as you love me as I hear you frequently

I stretch and I kick as I move around in silky warm waters

My bed rest is needed until I am born

So rub your belly as you pat my feet as I suck my fingers then

hang around and get more sleep

I'll be in your arms sooner than you think,

You anticipate the day when I will venture outside

But while you are waiting, tell my Daddy I said "Hi"

No worries, Mommy, I promise I won't be late

Tis Me

Early morning

Thankful to God I am

To start a new day, got lots to say

As I schedule out my day

Join me fore coffee, if you dare

I'll be at the bar drinking beer

To drink away my blues, hang around there till mid-afternoon

Head downtown to shop and play

On the way home; I purchase wine, flowers and herbs

Prep fore a quiet peaceful night,

Fore the moon is full and the air is sweet

I lie alone tonight

Till midnight

Then off into a very deep sleep

Tonight

Love me much, hold me close

Please don't rush, gently touch

Squeeze me tight, all through the night

Love it when you are near, no fear you are here

Knowing you care

Wipe away my tears

Arms and legs everywhere

Intertwine you're mine

Kisses and kisses and kisses

Oh my God, no more wishing

Sighing and crying, gasping for air

Hold me tight

Feelings are right; love me tonight

If not always then fore the moment

What the hell

You're my man tonight

Universal Love

Bright beam flashes across the sky

White lightning screams

High above the mountain top

Way above the tree tops

Soars across the mighty shores

Witnessed by cool summer breeze

Circles the heavens then gently lower me

Fore I am weak

There is earth below my feet

Steady above it

I float

A smile on my face

He touched my heart

The love of my life explored my universe

There he set my sun on fire

That burned through my soul

As he entered my twilight zone

Passionately we kissed

Forever I am under his spell - never to be released

Now that is what I call

LOVE

Viet Nam Veteran

Warrior, Soldier, Comrade, Tour in South Viet Nam; armed in
artillery, trained by the best, one color, one uniform, one flag
United in brotherhood – fore they are proud Marines
The United States Marine Corps ordered by
The President of the United States, Commander-in-Chief
United States of America, land of the free
Marines stand **STRONG, PROUD, BRAVE**
Fore they are everywhere land, sea and air
Sworn to protect, duty to serve **The FEW, PROUD, MARINES**
Boldly and courageously, eliminate the enemy, ward off
aggressors, strategically seize, defend and secure
Halt the suffering and torment of the innocent
Many American Soldiers proudly served in The Viet Nam War
I know one American Soldier, a Viet Nam Veteran
Whom I respect, honor and adore - fore he is:

My Brother - My Blood Brother
"Dawud Kaliym Muhammad"
aka
Corporal David D. Faison
United States Marine Corps
Machine Gun Squad Leader, Bravo Company
First Battalion, Active Duty
March 31, 1966 to August 29, 1969
Viet Nam Tour
July 1967 to August 1968
Presidential Ribbon and letter presented by
President Lyndon B. Johnson

Wealth

Enjoy the glimpse of a fallen star amid serene hills of wild
scented orchards. Sandy beaches or snowcapped mountains
Rainy days, no shoes, dance in the rain.
Hot summer days better yet, sun bathe.
Bare feet - hot coals - run like hell
Ocean waters cold as crap – stark-naked, skinny dip
Enjoy the moment and treasure your smiles
Waste not today, fore tomorrow may be too late.
Life is as pure gold fore, *"Your Life Is Your Wealth"*
Never let anyone tell you that you are useless, worthless or
anything else. You are not dead so smile instead. Rich in life to
sing, dance and pray. Never-you-mind fore who you are not, it
is who you are today and that is Damn Hot. So forsake not
self-fore others nor take their abuse; discard any users and
abusers like old worn out shoes. Stand tall, sing loud and yell
from the mountain-top fore, your voice shall be heard as you
sing, dance and pray. Live, love and enjoy life each and every
day; you only have one life so go out and play.
Don't waste time today's your lucky day
"Enjoy Your Wealth"

Who's The Finest?

Night cream, lightly on my face

Hair gel, looks like hell, rubbed throughout my hair

Bees' lotion soothes my body fore silky soft fine skin

Sliced cucumber, puffy eyes

Fright to sight, I need more sleep tonight

Sunrise, shower and bathe

Hurry, hurry; A.M. meeting

Stepping in red high heels, slim tight black dress

I must confess I look like a beautiful actress

Hair that flows, I am on the go; off to do my very best

I am CEO and President of my own establishment

So I must represent

Fore I'm a graduate of Princeton not Yale

Briefcase in hand and strategies in place

Ready to compete in this rat race

Though it is not the norm, you see

I was born to be Ms. President

Oh, give thanks to the LORD fore he is good

Fore his mercy endure forever

1 Chronicles 16:34

Widow

Black suit and black tie

Laid out flat and set aside

White shirt, dress shoes glisten and gleam fore they are new

Wrist watch and wedding band lay heavy on his dresser plate

Scents of his colognes lingered in our bedroom

I heard his voice it was clear as he whispered

I love you dear

His night robe left on the bathroom door, I touched it lightly
- never to be worn again -

On my knees I prayed

Lord please get me through this day

The black limousine arrived; silent ride, I cried

Quietly down the hill we went

Through the meadows and valleys

Tulips and daffodils of colors danced in harmony as they
swayed against the wind

Tears from angels fell from the sky

As sprinkles of rain collide with the sunlight

Grief leaves me cold and numb

I cannot believe this day has come

I wish this ride on no-one

Tears flow like Niagara Falls

I shiver and shake with sad thoughts

Declared his faith before death

Silenced like a lamb

His name inscribed in The Book of Life

The dust settled; last day on mother-earth

Foot-prints left in the dirt

Tombstone of gray granite signify dates on this planet

At the wake, sad songs I cannot take

Oh, how I mourn

What's left behind? A dark hole in my soul

Fore my heart was ripped out

When I buried the love of my life

I died with him on that dreadful night

Two souls dead instead of one

(The end of life is death)

Woman – Tis I Am

Tis I am many colors as the rainbow and I speak many
languages

Life's complexity lies within yet I manage to keep it together
from dusk till dawn, from beginning to end, all year long

I am woman, mother, doctor, consultant, chef and
household sanitation executive

As my splendid physique is unique, don't be deceived fore I am
not weak

I am slender, strong, courageous and bold

My intellect is challenged from day to day yet, I know many
things and I am not easily swayed

I am intelligent, independent, wise, complicated, and
opinionated

I house these things and so much more fore I am shelter,
cradle, and fortress

As my family expands through-out my community; I am loved
by so many I am sister, mother, neighbor and friend

As the day's end near there is more of me, fore I am enticing,
alluring, delicate and sweet

You see, "Tis I am the woman" who will captivate thee

Woman

I am strong

tall

intelligent

educated

independent

and wise

I am complicated

opinionated

sister

mother

wife

I am forgiving

tolerant

sweet

full of laughter

helper

shelter

life

I am woman

And I am

BOSS

Writings on the Wall

Move out and move on

It's time to get going as time has come to move along

Letting go saddens me; tears flow

Breaks my heart I could die

Fore what we had, did not survive

Blankets of darkness cover my past

Gray clouds weights heavy on my heart

Don't know how nor why; but time to move out

Time to move on and move along

The soft wind pushes against my back

Gives me strength to take these steps

To see what becomes of me

All is not lost fore we loved and laughed

Time to start a new path, as I want to hang on but I cannot lie

Deep in my heart I need to say goodbye

Don't ask why fore I'll cry as I leave great memories behind

Move out and move along

I must move on

Alone

XOXOXOXO's Valediction

He placed his hands on her waist and pulled her close

She placed her body within inches of his breath

She gently laid her head upon his chest as she felt his strength

The scent of his body raced through her soul

That very moment she knew he was God sent

If never to live another moment in time

She knew in her heart she had died in the arms loving a saint

He ran his fingers gently through her hair

With tears in his eyes

He kissed her lips

Whispered his love, then said

Goodbye

You and Me

Either you or me

Take you not me

Take me not you

Either way

One remains

Is it you

Or

Is it me?

Whoever is left?

Who will it be?

You or me

Let's see

Will you miss me?

Will I miss thee?

We will have to wait and see

You and me

Should beat the odds as we remain

United

About The Author

Patricia Faison-HesTer was born and raised on Shirley Street near Fairmount Avenue in Philadelphia Pennsylvania. Later she moved to Brewerytown of North Philadelphia.

Presently she resides in New Jersey.

Patricia is one of seven beautiful children born to Annie Lee Green-Faison-Medlock birthed five daughters and two sons.

Patricia is one of our newest writers to join the poetry circle and we congratulate her on her second published book:

Crazy Love

Printed in the United States
By Bookmasters